PARROTS

PARROTS

Mark J. Rauzon

A First Book

FRANKLIN WATTS *A Division of Grolier Publishing*
New York • London • Hong Kong • Sydney • Danbury, Connecticut

To my sister, Joyce Stevens

Frontispiece: Rainbow lories gather.
Photographs ©: Academy of Natural Sciences/VIREO: p. 38; Mark J. Rauzon:
pp. 19, 25; Photo Researchers: cover (Kenneth W. Fink), pp. 2 (J. M. Labat/Jacana),
13 (Toni Angermayer), 14 (Stephen Dalton), 17 (J. P. Ferrero/Jacana),20 (Gregory
G. Dimijian), 22 (Bill Bachman), 26 (Mitch Reardon), 29 (J. P. Ferrero/Jacana), 35
(Peter Skinner), 6 (both photos Jim Steinberg), 45 (Kenneth W. Fink), 48 (Tim
Davis), 51, 53 (Jacanana), 55 (Anthony Mercieca), 56 (Will & Deni McInty),
58 (Stephen J. Krasemann); Superstock, Inc.: pp. 8, 47; Visuals Unlimited: pp. 11
(John D. Cunningham), 32 (Ken Lucas), 42 (Kjell B. Sandved).

Library of Congress Cataloging-in-Publication Data

Rauzon, Mark J.
Parrots / Mark J. Rauzon.
p. cm. — (A First book)
Includes bibliographical references and index.
Summary: Describes different kinds of parrots, including parakeets,
macaws, cockatoos, and lovebirds.
ISBN 0-531-20244-5 (lib. bdg.) — ISBN 0-531-15815-2 (pbk.)
1. Parrots—Juvenile literature. I. Title. II. Series.
QL696.P7R37 1996
598.7'1—dc20   96-3377356

CIP
AC

CONTENTS

PARROTS

The parrot's thick, hooked beak comes in handy for cracking nuts.

BIRDS OF A FEATHER

Parrots have feathers of magnificent colors, make terrific pets, and can mimic human speech. That's why they are among the best-known birds in the world. Relatives of the parrots include parakeets, budgerigars, lories, lorikeets, macaws, cockatoos, cockatiels, keas, rosellas, and lovebirds. More than three hundred different species, or kinds, of birds can be called parrots.

Parrots are perhaps most easily recognized by their distinctive thick, hooked beaks. The top and bottom halves of their curved beaks fit together perfectly. Large jaw muscles in their large heads operate these powerful beaks. Parrots use their beaks to carve nest holes in rotten wood, dig hard dirt, crack heavy seeds and nuts, and give tender nibbles during courtship.

A parrot eating is a fascinating sight. They use their powerful beaks and flexible tongues in combination with their feet to hold and crack open hard food like nuts with great skill. While other birds, like hawks, lower their heads to their feet, which grip their food, parrots lift food up to their beaks, using their feet as hands. When they hold food, most parrots are "left-footed."

Parrots are the best climbers of all birds. Unlike any other bird, they brace and move themselves on tree limbs by grasping branches with their bills. Parrots have zygodactylous feet (two curved toes pointing forward and two curved toes pointing backward). This type of foot enables parrots to grasp tree branches better than other birds, which have three toes pointing forward and only one pointing backward.

In trees, parrots are extraordinary acrobats, hanging upside down or climbing up a jungle vine. On the ground, however, most parrots are awkward, waddling from side to side, with the feet turned in.

A blue-and-yellow macaw climbs using its feet and bill.

Parrots are rainbow-colored birds. Most parrots are emerald green on the wings and back, but their heads and underparts are red, yellow, blue, or purple. Their ornate plumage makes parrots some of the world's most beautiful birds. Despite their many bright colors, they are very hard to spot in the shadows of the treetops where they live.

The parrot's beautiful feathers require much care. Parrots preen themselves and each other with their agile tongues and beaks. Throughout their plumage are special feathers called powder down. These feathers can crumble into a waterproof dust, which parrots rub into their feathers to help remove body oil and dirt.

An adaptable and lively group of birds, parrots are very social. Nibbling each other around the head is part of feather maintenance and helps to build and maintain the bond between birds. They usually mate for life and stick together in pairs, which sometimes join together in large flocks.

The best example of a social parrot is the lovebird, a small, short-tailed parrot from southern Africa. Lovebirds display complete harmony by bathing, eating, calling, and sleeping together. It has been said that if one of a pair of lovebirds disappears, the other sometimes dies, as if from loneliness.

A pair of lovebirds preen.

An Amazon parrot takes flight.

CHAPTER TWO

"POLLY WANT A CRACKER?"

Parrots are the noisiest of all the animals in the forest. *Raak, kraak, raaaah, kwaaa, aa* are the sounds parrots make flying over the forest canopy, commuting from their favorite feeding areas to their nesting or roosting trees. They stay in constant communication with each other through sounds that range from ear-splitting screeches to quiet twittering and chattering. Parrots are well known for mimicking human speech and jungle sounds. They very rarely copy any other bird or parrot calls in the wild.

Some parrots, though not all, have the ability to imitate the human voice. "Talking" is an extension of the many loud noises that parrots make. And since large parrots live up to seventy-five years, they have a lot of time to learn. Most trained parrots have a vocabulary of less than 20 words, but the most talkative bird known—a parakeet from Britain named Sparkie Williams who lived in the late 1950s—had a vocabulary of 531 words.

The African gray parrot is highly prized for its remarkable ability to copy sounds. One American researcher in animal behavior taught an African gray named Alex to make requests like "Tickle me," "I want popcorn," and "Go away!" Although some parrots are intelligent and can give the impression that they are communicating, there is little evidence that they understand what they say. However, the way Alex puts together sentences indicates he may be able to think and not just imitate his trainers.

The parrot's ability to imitate the human voice has made for some strange situations in history. A parrot discovered in the late 1700s in South America by the great German explorer Alexander von Humboldt spoke the words of a tribe of South American Indians that had ceased to exist. The parrot had outlived all the people and was the last speaker of a "dead" language. In an unusual modern-day story, the only witness to a crime

The African gray parrot is well known for its intelligence.

was a talking parrot, which uttered the name of a possible suspect to the police.

Some smarter parrots can be trained to do tricks. Trainers have been able to mold natural behaviors that the birds exhibit in the wild into performances by reinforcing the birds with food. Pedaling bicycles, counting nuts, ringing bells, pulling hoops, and even talking are extensions of natural behaviors in the forest.

Different types of parrots do certain tricks better than others. Cockatoos can climb and hang better than macaws, which can walk better on the ground. Once trained, however, the birds must keep on performing regularly or they will become bored and may pull out their feathers.

Parrots have fascinated and entertained people throughout history. In ancient South America, people domesticated parrots long before history began to be recorded. As early as 400 B.C., the Greeks kept blossom-headed parakeets as pets. Alexander the Great was responsible for bringing parrots to Europe from the Far East in 323 B.C. The Alexandrine parakeet is named in

A trained cockatoo pedals a minibicycle at a local fair.

his honor. African gray parrots entertained Roman nobility and were kept in silver and tortoiseshell cages. One Roman emperor, Elagabalus, fed parrot bodies to the lions and consumed the brains himself.

When Christopher Columbus returned from the Americas at the end of the 1400s, he showed off parrots and macaws in triumphal parades through Spain. Parrots became the birds of royalty; they were gifts to kings and queens who financed expeditions. Examples of parrot species named after royalty include the king parrot, the Queen of Bavaria conure, the princess parrot, the duchess lorikeet, the cardinal lory, the regent parrot, and the imperial Amazon. The oldest known specimen is a stuffed African gray parrot, the cherished pet of a British duchess who lived in the 1700s. A fascination with parrots continues to this day all over the world.

The colorful king parrot from Australia was named after royalty.

ALL IN THE FAMILY

Parrots are native to every continent except Europe. Australia is home to more species and more unusual types of parrots than any other continent. Many parrots live in South America. About a dozen kinds of parrots live in Africa and in India. At one time there were two kinds of parrots that lived in the United States. One has become extinct and the other barely survives

Although parrots are most common in the world's tropical regions, they can also be found in the cold mountains. Keas, for example, which live in the New Zealand mountains, gather on rock ledges in the high country to bask in the sun, but they also may roll in the snow.

Unlike most parrots, keas of New Zealand live in snowy climates.

The best-known relative of the parrot is the common pet parakeet, but few people know its real name. The common pet parakeet is the budgerigar, or the "budgie." They are almost as popular as cats and dogs and are found in pet stores around the world.

Parakeets were first brought to England from Australia in 1840. Demand for them increased as people discovered how hardy, attractive, and gentle the birds were. Although few could afford the first imported birds, people learned to breed them in captivity. Prices dropped and parakeets of all colors became more common.

Unfortunately, parrots, including parakeets, have been known to carry a life-threatening virus that can be passed on to humans. The flulike disease called psittacosis, or parrot fever, was discovered in a study conducted in 1929 and 1930. Parrot fever, now easily controlled by antibiotics, seems not to have affected the pet trade.

Today's pet-store parakeets are very different in color and behavior from their Australian cousins. In the wild, parakeets are probably the most abundant kind of parrot. They wander in spectacular flocks throughout the dry

Crimson-fronted parakeets peep out of their nest.

A rainbow lorikeet feeds from flowers.

inland areas in search of food and water. When they find sufficient quantities of each, they settle down and nest.

Nearly all parrots and parakeets nest in tree holes, often made by woodpeckers and then enlarged by parrots. These birds do not search out nest material. Instead, they shave punky wood from inside the hole to use to cushion their eggs.

The golden-shouldered parrot, however, nests among insects. They dig a hole in Australian termite mounds. Termite larvae keep the nest clean by eating the chicks' waste matter. The birds benefit from the arrangement because predators are less likely to smell the nest and harm the baby chicks.

In the wild, parakeets live three to four years and lay up to six eggs a year. They can produce as many as twenty-four chicks during their lifetime. In captivity, budgies have lived to twenty-one years of age.

It is easy to tell a parrot from a parakeet. Parrots have short, square tails and rounded wings, and parakeets have long, tapered tails and narrow wings. Parakeets are swift flyers. Parrots, with their large, broad wings, fly a little slower.

Lorikeets and lories are like parakeets and parrots, but they have a different type of tongue. These kinds of parrots have brushlike tongues designed to sweep pollen and nectar from flowers. Their weak beaks nibble open flowers, but they cannot crack seeds. Because of their unique diet, these birds do not thrive in captivity.

It is easy to tell a lory from a lorikeet. Lorikeets have narrow wings and pointed tails like parakeets, while lories have square tails like parrots.

Lories and lorikeets are some of the most beautifully colored birds. The brilliant plumage of the ornate lorikeet shines in the sun, and perhaps helps to hide them in the flowers where they feed. About one hundred species of lorikeets and lories live in Australia, New Guinea, and many islands in the South Pacific.

Parrots come in all sizes. Pygmy parrots of New Guinea are the smallest—just 4 inches (10 cm) long and no bigger than sparrows. They climb under branches and tree trunks searching for plants to eat and are hard to see because of their secretive habits.

Just a bit bigger are the hanging parrots, which sleep upside down like bats. These tiny birds hang by their feet and claws under treetop branches in the rain forests.

A fig parrot munches on figs.

Tiger parrots are medium-sized green birds with black stripes, a combination of colors that makes them hard to see in the treetops of tropical mountain forests. They stick close together and rarely fly far.

Fig parrots are small and plump with large heads. As the name implies, fig parrots eat the tiny seeds of figs. They are like gardeners, scattering seeds around the rain forest. As is the case with many birds, fruit seeds go through the fig parrot's digestive system intact and are deposited in the tops of other trees. A new tree may grow far away from where the fig parrot originally ate the fruit.

Vulturine parrots are crow-sized fig eaters. They look like vultures because they have a small, featherless head to allow them to eat figs without soiling their plumage with sticky fig juice. Hunted for their striking red and black plumes for use in costumes and head-dresses, the vulturine parrot, which lives in New Guinea, is now rare.

Cockatoos, Cockatiels, and Kakapos

Australia is home to sixteen species of cockatoos. Cockatoos are large parrots with square tails and feather crests that can be raised or lowered depending on the mood of the bird. Mainly white, black, or gray, they are the least colorful parrots. The colors under their crests, however, can be shocking pink or yellow.

Cockatoos hang upside down and extend their crests to impress their mates. A courting male walks along a branch by placing his feet carefully, bobbing and swaying his head in figure eights and chattering softly all the while. The male and the female preen each other and touch bills before mating. She lays two eggs in a tree hole and sits on, or incubates, them for three weeks. When the young are hatched, they are blind

and featherless. They are fed a liquid diet, regurgitated—brought up from the crop, or stomach—by both parents.

The red-tailed cockatoo has a black body with vivid red swatches in its tail that flash in the sun. The bird takes baths in the wet leaves after a rain and flies around on moonlit nights in northern Australia.

The largest cockatoo species is the palm cockatoo, found in the rain forests of New Guinea and northeast Australia. The slate-gray–colored birds have pink faces, which can blush dark red when they get excited. Nothing excites them more than having their nests raided by bird collectors. These spectacular birds can fetch thousands of dollars on the black market. Unfortunately, when the trees they nest in are cut down to get the valuable baby birds, the parents have nowhere else to nest.

The galah, or roseate cockatoo, is a large gray and pink bird with a small white crest. While many Australians favor the galah as a pet, farmers consider them pests because of the damage large flocks of them

Courting cockatoos rest on a tree limb.

can do to crops. After the breeding season is over, mated pairs join in flocks numbering in the hundreds. They become wanderers, roaming the forests and farmlands eating seeds, fruits, berries, and nuts. A flock's loud shrieking announces its presence overhead.

Cockatiel means "little cockatoo" in Portuguese. Cockatiels are easy to distinguish from cockatoos because they have tapering tails like parakeets. Cockatiels became popular cage birds over the last few decades because they make gentle, affectionate, and easy-to-care-for pets. Slightly larger than budgerigars, they have feather crests, an orange patch on their yellow faces, and light-gray bodies with white wing bars. Like budgies, they also form large flocks, which roam the dry interior of Australia. Their gray and yellow coloration blends into the shadows and ground cover where they feed.

Another interesting Australian bird, the eclectus parrot, had scientists confused for many years. Because males and females are different colors—males are green and females are red—they were thought to be two different species.

Crimson rosellas are brilliantly colored small parrots that live in forests near towns in northeastern Australia. They feed on seeds, fruits, and nuts that they

Cockatiels make popular pets.

A male eclectus (left) and female eclectus (right) differ in color.

search for on or near the ground. Pairs seek tree holes in which to breed, making a nest of powdered wood and laying several round white eggs. The name *rosella* comes from early Australian colonists who saw the birds in a village called Rose Hill and dubbed them the "rose hillers." The name was shortened into a unique Australian name for a unique Australian bird.

Of all the birds, there is none stranger than the kakapo, the owl-parrot of New Zealand. "One of the most wonderful perhaps of all living birds" is how one researcher described the kakapo. Another composed a short poem after observing the rare kakapo in the wild:

> A parrot that booms by the light of the moon,
> An owl that eats grass and cries like a loon,
> A flightless green what-not that waddles around,
> Luffing and lolling in a hole underground.

Originally, the kakapo was thought to be an owl. Just like an owl, its eyes face forward instead of to the side, as in most other birds, and its beak is partially hidden by feathers. The kakapo lives in an underground burrow and comes out only at night to waddle among the grasses and herbs that it eats. In the breeding sea-

The kakapo is one of the world's rarest birds.

son, the male calls in females by beating his very short wings against his chest—a behavior called "booming."

The females are attracted to the flat areas where males boom. These dancing arenas are called "leks." Females mate with the males that boom the loudest. The mating pair is not permanent, and the males do not help take care of the young. Females reach breeding condition every two to four years and lay one to two eggs. It is a slow process to create a kakapo, but the long-lived bird can raise several young during its life.

The kakapo is the heaviest parrot. It is also the only flightless parrot: with its short wings, the kakapo can only glide downhill. It is certainly one of the rarest birds in the world. Because weasels and cats eat the ground-nesting kakapo, only fifty remain.

With a little help from the New Zealand Wildlife Service, the kakapo may begin to return from the brink of extinction. Birds have been moved from islands where cats live to islands free of predators to give them a chance to breed. If these efforts fail, the fabulous kakapo could soon become extinct.

Other rare and endangered parrots nest on the ground. The rock parrot nests under beach stones just above the ocean high-tide mark. Night parrots live in the deserts of South Australia and come out only after dark. Ground parrots, colored green and yellow, are rare in the grasslands of southern Australia. Rats, cats, sheep, and cattle have had a destructive impact on these endangered ground-dwelling parrots.

The Real Macaws

With their long, sweeping tails and the strongest bite in the bird world, macaws are the most impressive of all the parrots. Spanish and Portuguese explorers to the Americas took macaws back to Europe in the early 1500s. Ever since then, people have wanted them as pets.

Sixteen species of macaws live in tropical forests from Mexico to Argentina in South America. The largest macaw, the hyacinth macaw, weighs about 3 pounds (1.4 kg) and has a length of 3 feet (91 cm). Their pointed tails are as long as their royal-blue bodies. The smallest macaws weigh about 1 pound (.5 kg) and live on the Caribbean islands.

The beautiful and intelligent macaws are becoming increasingly popular as pets. Unfortunately, they do not

breed as well in captivity as some of the smaller parrots and parakeets. To satisfy the pet-bird market, collectors take a certain number of macaws from their tropical homes. The most valuable parrots in the pet bird trade, macaws may sell for thousands of dollars each. Due to this profitable macaw trade, some of the most magnificent species are growing rare.

Some parrot collectors cut down the nest trees to get at the nestlings. Collectors ship them out of the rain forests to cities in other parts of the world. Only a few chicks survive the long-distance travel to pet stores in the United States and Europe. Most die along the way, and the animal populations in the wild suffer the loss of hard-to-find nesting trees. Several hundred years of parrot trade has taken its toll on wildlife, and many species are threatened with extinction in their tropical homelands.

Eight species of macaws are endangered or threatened. The rarest, Spix's macaw, is down to just a few wild birds. Recently, an international law called for the end of importing wild birds. That law is beginning to have an effect. Many birds for sale in pet shops are

The deep-blue hyacinth macaw is the largest of all parrots.

raised in captivity, but some rare macaws are still smuggled into the country.

Luckily, the blue-and-yellow macaw is still one of the most common macaw species in South American rain forests. Out of one hundred pairs of macaws in the wild, only ten to twenty will mate in a year and only five to fifteen chicks will survive. Two eggs are laid in the hollow core of a palm tree. If all goes well, two chicks hatch. The first one out of its egg has an advantage; it gets more food than its smaller brother or sister and so grows faster. Usually the smaller bird starves to death because parents are unable to find enough food for two growing chicks. Parents groom the surviving chick to remove ticks and lice and help spread their natural oils on their bright feathers.

Like most parrots, macaws need large dead trees in which to dig their nests. There are few sites available since dead wood quickly rots in the hot and humid rain forests. The practice of building artificial nests out of plastic pipe to stop the population decline of macaws has had some success. The macaws readily use the man-made nests.

After the macaws hatch their eggs, biologists take the smaller chick from the nest. Since the weaker one

Two blue-and-yellow macaws at play screech
and swoop around each other.

would die, it is hand-fed until it can fly on its own. These young are dependent on humans for three months. During that time, they must be protected from rainstorms, hungry weasels, and vicious flies. When the young macaws finally leave their adoptive parents, they join their older siblings screeching in the treetops.

Macaws eat flowers, leaves, the pulp of fruits, and a variety of seeds and nuts, including Brazil nuts, which they crack with their massive ivory-colored bills. Much of the macaw's food has a bitter taste. Plants make chemicals that taste unpleasant to keep animals from eating the seeds. Macaws and other parrots have found a way to eat all the bitter fruit they want. In certain areas of South America, they eat clay from the river-banks to calm their upset stomachs and neutralize the toxins in their food. Salts and minerals in the clay also help improve their diet.

At a bend in the river in the Amazon jungle, flocks of scarlet macaws swoop into the treetops. They fly in pairs and live in family groups. They are joined by red-

Red-and-green macaws have distinctive stripes on their faces.

A flying scarlet macaw displays its brilliant plumage.

and-green macaws. Squawking loudly and looking out for predators, they all drop to the clay and begin digging into the dirt with their heavy bills. Biologists watch from a hidden place, looking for birds they know.

Each red-and-green macaw has lines of feathers on its face that are unique. Specialists can read them like fingerprints and identify individuals. By studying them individually, they can tell how often they eat clay, when they breed, and how long they live. They have also found that macaws eat more toxic seeds and clay in the driest period of the year when other fresh foods are not available.

In the wild, macaws live between thirty and forty-five years and probably die from disease, parasites, or harpy eagle attacks. They mate for life and are constant companions so there is always a pair of eyes watching for predators or human hunters. When they suspect danger, they fly off screeching loudly, alerting every animal within earshot. In captivity, where life is safer but far less exciting, macaws can live to seventy years.

PARROTS IN DANGER

Although many parrot species are threatened with extinction, some other species have been so numerous at one time or another as to be considered pests. Examples include monk parakeets, rose-ringed parakeets, and keas.

One of the hardiest kinds of parrots, the monk parakeet has successfully established itself in the United States after accidentally escaping captivity. The birds probably escaped from damaged cages shipped from Argentina, where the birds are native. They survive as far north as Chicago, Illinois, because of the many backyard bird feeders. People first thought that monk parakeets would become a problem in the

Monk parakeets are very social birds,
gathering in flocks of one hundred or more.

orchards and fields. Monk parakeets, however, have never reached large enough populations to do significant damage.

Rose-ringed parakeets live in Africa and Asia, as well as Hawaii, where they were introduced. They have also been introduced to southern England, where the successful and invasive birds are thriving and taking over the nest holes of native birds. In India, they are very common in city parks and gardens, where they nest under tiled roofs and in cavities in dead trees. Flocks of up to 250 invade millet fields and orchards, in spite of scarecrows posted on platforms around the fields.

Keas, unlike most parrots, have been known to eat meat. They have a reputation for killing sheep and, for over a century, at least 150,000 of the birds were killed by New Zealand bounty hunters. Keas are now protected. They have become fearless, scavenging near ski slopes, parking lots, and farms and occasionally sampling the rubber windshield wipers of cars.

Many other parrot species, however, are so scarce as to be considered endangered. Today, thirty species of parrots are threatened with extinction from two main causes: capture for the pet trade and habitat destruc-

In populated areas, keas can prove themselves nuisances.

tion. Some of those species include Puerto Rican parrots, turquoise parrots, and golden conures.

In 1975, Puerto Rican parrots were down to thirteen wild birds. Through active conservation measures, their numbers have tripled in recent years. While the population increase is welcome news, habitat destruction may prevent the species from fully recovering.

Turquoise parrots are limited to the dry forests of Australia, where they are increasingly rare. Though not yet endangered, increased logging in their habitat could threaten their populations with extinction.

Also rare are the golden conures, found only in a small section of Brazil near the mouth of the Amazon River. They nest in treetops and feed on fruit and nectar.

The last thick-billed parrot disappeared from southern Arizona in 1935. Luckily, thick-billed parrots continued to exist in Mexico, and some of these birds were reintroduced back into Arizona. The effort to bring birds back to the United States began with twenty-nine wild parrots that the U.S. Fish and Wildlife Service

Thick-billed parrots used to inhabit the southwestern United States.

Carolina parakeets now exist only in paintings.

recently seized from bird smugglers. When the birds were released in the mountains, however, they had problems locating food and avoiding predators like hawks. Without experienced parrots to guide them, the newly released birds got lost or eaten.

It is hoped that the thick-billed parrot will learn how to live in its old neighborhood again. Perhaps sometime soon this emerald-green parrot with a scarlet shoulder patch and a red forehead will return to the forests. Perhaps sometime soon it will be spotted in the wild, getting covered with sticky sap in the process of using its thick bill to wedge open pine cones to get at the seeds.

For many other kinds of parrots, it is too late. The last Cuban red macaw was shot in 1864. The last Norfolk Island parrot or kaka died around 1851 in a cage in London almost on the other side of the world from its home. And the only parakeet native to the United States, the Carolina parakeet, did not survive.

Carolina parakeets were shot because they were pests to fruit growers in the orchards of the southern United States. As early as 1831, bird lover and artist John James Audubon wrote that they were rapidly disappearing. As soon as people realized that the yellow-

A red-lored parrot perches on a tree trunk
in a Costa Rican rain forest.

headed parakeets were growing rare, the problem was made worse by a rush to collect the last ones. Because these birds gathered in large flocks, it was easy to shoot many at one time, so their numbers speedily decreased. The last one died in a zoo in 1918.

Parrots are popular perhaps in part because they remind us of ourselves. They stand up straight and use their feet like hands, they can mimic human speech, they can live as long as we do, and they can be friendly. And they are also beautiful. While these qualities may endear parrots to us, parrots have suffered from our desires to own them.

With the destruction of their forest homes, the cutting down of their nest trees, and the loss of their babies to smugglers, many parrots are in danger of extinction. To keep any more parrot species from becoming extinct, we must ensure that only captive-raised parrots become pets and that their habitats are protected so that parrots can continue to liven the jungle and forests with their outrageous cries, colors, and antics.

FOR FURTHER READING

Burnie, David. *Bird*. New York: Knopf Books for Young Readers, 1988.

Dunnahoo, Terry. *The Lost Parrots of America*. New York: Macmillan, 1989.

Gabin, Martin. *Your First Parrot*. Neptune, N.J.: TFH Publications, 1991.

Haley, Neale. *Birds for Pets and Pleasure*. New York: Delacorte, 1981.

Harris, Alan, ed. *Birds*. New York: Dorling Kindersley, 1993.

Leon, Vicki. *Parrots, Macaws, and Cockatoos*. San Luis Obispo, Calif.: Blake Publishing, 1989.

Stone, Lynn M. *Parrots*. Vero Beach, Fla.: Rourke Corporation, 1993.

Wolter, Annette. *African Gray Parrots*. Hauppauge, N.Y.: Barron, 1987.

INDEX

Italicized page numbers refer to illustrations.

ABOUT THE AUTHOR

Mark J. Rauzon is an environmental consultant and a writer-photographer who travels widely. He has worked as a biologist for the U.S. Fish and Wildlife Service and served as chair of the Pacific Seabird Group. Mr. Rauzon is the author of several children's books about animals, including *Seabirds* for Franklin Watts. He lives in Oakland, California.